HISTORY'S MOST INFLUENTIAL
WOMEN

FROM THE Early 1900s TO THE Mid-1900s

Marie Stopes to Mother Teresa

EDITED BY KATHLEEN KUIPER

Britannica®
Educational Publishing

IN ASSOCIATION WITH

ROSEN
EDUCATIONAL SERVICES

Published in 2024 by Britannica Educational Publishing
(a trademark of Encyclopædia Britannica, Inc.)
in association with Rosen Educational Services, LLC
2544 Clinton Street, Buffalo, NY 14224.

Copyright © 2024 Encyclopædia Britannica, Inc. Britannica, Encyclopædia Britannica, and the Thistle logo are registered trademarks of Encyclopædia Britannica, Inc. All rights reserved.

Rosen Educational Services materials copyright © 2024 Rosen Educational Services, LLC. All rights reserved.

Distributed exclusively by Rosen Educational Services.
For a listing of additional Britannica Educational Publishing titles, call toll free (800) 237-9932.

First Edition

Britannica Educational Publishing
Michael I. Levy: Executive Editor
Marilyn L. Barton: Senior Coordinator, Production Control
Steven Bosco: Director, Editorial Technologies
Lisa S. Braucher: Senior Producer and Data Editor
Yvette Charboneau: Senior Copy Editor
Kathy Nakamura: Manager, Media Acquisition
Kathleen Kuiper: Manager, Arts and Culture

Editor: Kathleen Kuiper
Book design: Michael Flynn

Photo credits: Cover https://commons.wikimedia.org/wiki/File:NPG_75_82_Earhart.jpg; p. 14 https://commons.wikimedia.org/wiki/File:George_Charles_Beresford_-_Virginia_Woolf_in_1902_-_Restoration.jpg; p. 28 https://commons.wikimedia.org/wiki/File:Eleanor_Roosevelt_in_New_York_City_-_NARA_-_195413.jpg; p. 38 https://commons.wikimedia.org/wiki/File:Soong_May-ling_giving_a_special_radio_broadcast.jpg; p. 41 https://commons.wikimedia.org/wiki/File:Amelia_Earhart_LOC_hec.40747.jpg; p. 46 https://commons.wikimedia.org/wiki/File:Golda_Meir_03265u.jpg; p. 50 https://commons.wikimedia.org/wiki/File:Marlene_Dietrich_02b.jpg; p. 60 https://commons.wikimedia.org/wiki/File:Mother_Teresa_(49096605572).jpg.

Cataloging-in-Publication Data

Names: Kuiper, Kathleen.
Title: From the early 1900s to the mid-1900s—Marie Stopes to Mother Theresa / edited by Kathleen Kuiper.
Description: New York : Britannica Educational Publishing, in Association with Rosen Educational Services. 2024. | Series: History's most influential women | Includes glossary and index.
Identifiers: ISBN 9781641900782 (library bound) | ISBN 9781641900775 (pbk) | ISBN 9781641900799 (ebook)
Subjects: LCSH: Women--Biography--Juvenile literature. | Women--History--20th century--Juvenile literature. | Women--History--Juvenile literature.
Classification: LCC HQ1123.K87 2024 | DDC 920.72 B--dc23

Manufactured in the United States of America

CPSIA Compliance Information: Batch #CWBRIT24. For further information contact Rosen Publishing at 1-800-237-9932.

CONTENTS

Introduction 4
Marie Stopes 6
Virginia Woolf 7
Coco Chanel 23
Eleanor Roosevelt 25
Karen Horney 30
Martha Graham 32
Soong Mei-ling 37
Amelia Earhart 40
Irène Joliot-Curie 42
Golda Meir 45
Marlene Dietrich 48
Simone Weil .52
Katherine Dunham 53
Dorothy Crowfoot Hodgkin 55
Mother Teresa 58
Glossary 62
For More Information 63
Index 64

INTRODUCTION

"A woman is like a tea bag. You never know how strong it is until it's in hot water."
—*Eleanor Roosevelt (1884–1962)*

The world is filled with fascinating women, and each woman has her own compelling story. This book contains profiles of striking individuals who serve as outstanding representatives of their gender. It covers many of the most noteworthy, influential women from around the globe who lived and made their mark between the early 1900s and the mid-1900s.

Most of these women managed to flourish in the face of adversity, and some of the individuals featured in this title came to the fore by helping to empower other women. For example, Marie Stopes advocated the use of birth control in England as a way to improve women's health. In Germany, the psychoanalyst Karen Horney promoted a new, female perspective in a field that had been dominated by male ideas.

Some of the other women in this book are noted for their humanitarianism. As first lady, Eleanor Roosevelt was dedicated to elevating the role of women and achieving equal rights in American society. She also sought to influence human rights around the world through her work with the United Nations. Similarly, Mother Teresa adopted an international, humanitarian mission. Her work through the Roman Catholic church focused on direct service to people living in poverty.

The early 1900s was a period of major milestones for women. The record-setting aviator Amelia Earhart became the first woman to fly across the Atlantic Ocean alone. Golda Meir became the first female prime minister in Israel. The chemists Irène Joliot-Curie and Dorothy Crowfoot Hodgkin added their accomplishments to the growing list of female scientists, and their work was recognized with Nobel Prizes.

Then there are the women who have left their mark on humankind's collective creative history. Virginia Woolf authored many experimental novels and literary masterpieces. She also produced a wealth of essays that examined a variety of artistic and social topics, including the creative limitations society imposes on women.

Several distinguished women in this book entertained and enlightened the public. In this period, Martha Graham developed the art of modern dance, and Katherine Dunham explored dance performance as cultural expression. Marlene Dietrich was a grand dame of the screen. Her performances became the watermark by which other actresses have measured their own careers.

The influence of these women, and the others profiled in this book, reverberates throughout the ages. Their leadership, scientific research, and artistic vision have served to enrich, enlighten, and shape modern society. These amazing and influential individuals have given all of us, men and women alike, something to admire and strive for in our own lives.

MARIE STOPES

(b. Oct. 15, 1880, Edinburgh, Scot.—d. Oct. 2, 1958, near Dorking, Surrey, Eng.)

Marie Stopes (in full Marie Charlotte Carmichael Stopes) was an advocate of birth control who, in 1921, founded the United Kingdom's first instructional clinic for contraception. Although her clinical work, writings, and speeches evoked violent opposition, especially from Roman Catholics, she greatly influenced the Church of England's gradual relaxation (from 1930) of its stand against birth control.

Stopes grew up in a wealthy, educated family; her father was an architect, her mother a scholar of Shakespeare and an advocate for the education of women. Stopes obtained a science degree (1902) from University College, London, which she completed in only two years. She went on to do postgraduate studies in paleobotany (fossil plants), earning a doctorate from the University of Munich in 1904. That same year she became an assistant lecturer of botany at the University of Manchester. She specialized in fossil plants and the problems of coal mining.

She married her first husband, a botanist named Reginald Ruggles Gates, in 1911. Stopes would later assert that her marriage was unconsummated and that she knew little about sex when she first married. Her failed marriage and its eventual annulment in 1916 played a large role in determining her future career, causing her to turn her attention to the issues of sex, marriage, and childbirth and their meaning in society. She initially saw birth control as an aid to marriage fulfillment and as a means to save women from the physical strain of excessive childbearing. In this regard for quality of life of the individual woman, she differed from most other early leaders of the birth-control movement, who were more concerned with social good, such as the elimination of overpopulation and poverty.

In 1918, Stopes married Humphrey Verdon Roe, cofounder of the A.V. Roe aircraft firm, who also had strong interests in the birth-control movement. He helped her in the crusade that she then began. Their original birth-control clinic—designed to educate women about the few methods of birth control available to them—was founded three years later, in the working-class Holloway district of London. That same year she became founder and president of the Society for Constructive Birth Control, a platform from which she spoke widely about the benefits of married women having healthy, desired babies. In the meantime, she wrote *Married Love* and *Wise Parenthood* (both 1918), which were widely translated. Her *Contraception: Its Theory, History and Practice* (1923) was, when it first appeared, the most comprehensive treatment of the subject. After World War II, she promoted birth control in East Asian countries.

VIRGINIA WOOLF
(b. Jan. 25, 1882, London, Eng.—d. March 28, 1941, near Rodmell, Sussex)

English writer Virginia Woolf is noted mainly for a group of novels that through their nonlinear approaches to narrative, exerted a major influence on the genre. While she is best known for her novels, especially *Mrs. Dalloway* (1925) and *To the Lighthouse* (1927), Woolf also wrote pioneering essays on artistic theory, literary history, women's writing, and the politics of power. A fine stylist, she experimented with several forms of biographical writing, composed painterly short fictions, and sent to her friends and family a lifetime of brilliant letters.

Early Life and Influences

Born Adeline Virginia Stephen, she was the child of ideal Victorian parents. Her father, Leslie Stephen, was an eminent literary figure and the first editor (1882–91) of the *Dictionary of National Biography*. Her mother, Julia Jackson, possessed great beauty and a reputation for saintly self-sacrifice; she also had prominent social and artistic connections, which included Julia Margaret Cameron, her aunt and one of the greatest portrait photographers of the 19th century. Both Jackson's first husband, Herbert Duckworth, and Stephen's first wife, a daughter of the novelist William Makepeace Thackeray, had died unexpectedly, leaving her three children and him one.

Julia Jackson Duckworth and Leslie Stephen married in 1878, and four children followed: Vanessa (born 1879), Thoby (born 1880), Virginia (born 1882), and Adrian (born 1883). While these four children banded together against their older half siblings, loyalties shifted among them. Virginia was jealous of Adrian for being their mother's favorite. At age nine, she was the genius behind a family newspaper, the *Hyde Park Gate News*, that often teased Vanessa and Adrian. Vanessa mothered the others, especially Virginia, but the dynamic between need (Virginia's) and aloofness (Vanessa's) sometimes expressed itself as rivalry between Virginia's art of writing and Vanessa's art of painting.

The Stephen family made summer migrations from their London town house near Kensington Gardens to the rather disheveled Talland House on the rugged Cornwall coast. That annual relocation structured Virginia's childhood world in terms of opposites: city and country, winter and summer, repression and freedom, fragmentation and wholeness. Her neatly divided, predictable world ended, however, when her mother died in 1895 at age 49. Virginia, at 13, ceased writing amusing accounts of family news. Almost a year passed before she wrote a cheerful letter to her brother Thoby. She was just emerging from depression when, in 1897, her half sister Stella Duckworth died at age 28, an event Virginia noted in her diary as "impossible to write of." Then in 1904, after her father died, Virginia had a nervous breakdown.

While Virginia was recovering, Vanessa supervised the Stephen children's move to the bohemian Bloomsbury section of London. There the siblings lived independent of their Duckworth half brothers, free to pursue studies, to paint or write, and to entertain. Leonard Woolf dined with them in November 1904, just before sailing to Ceylon (now Sri Lanka) to become a colonial administrator. Soon the Stephens hosted weekly gatherings of radical young people, including Clive Bell, Lytton Strachey, and John Maynard Keynes, all later to achieve fame as, respectively, an art critic, a biographer, and an economist.

Then, after a family excursion to Greece in 1906, Thoby died of typhoid fever. He was 26. Virginia grieved but did not slip into depression. She overcame the loss of Thoby and the "loss" of Vanessa, who became engaged to Bell just after Thoby's death, through writing. Vanessa's marriage (and perhaps Thoby's absence) helped transform conversation at the avant-garde gatherings of what came to be known as the Bloomsbury group into irreverent, sometimes bawdy repartee that inspired Virginia to exercise her wit publicly, even while privately she was writing her poignant "Reminiscences"—about her childhood and her lost mother—which was published in 1908. Viewing Italian art that summer, she committed herself to creating in language "some kind of whole made of shivering fragments," to capturing "the flight of the mind."

Early Fiction

Virginia Stephen determined in 1908 to "re-form" the novel by creating a holistic form embracing aspects of life that were "fugitive" from the Victorian novel. While writing anonymous reviews for the *Times Literary Supplement* and other journals, she experimented with such a novel, which she called *Melymbrosia*. In November 1910, Roger Fry, a new friend of the Bells, launched the exhibit "Manet and the Post-Impressionists," which introduced radical European art to the London bourgeoisie. Virginia was at once outraged over the attention that painting garnered and intrigued by the possibility of borrowing from the likes of artists Paul Cézanne and Pablo Picasso. As Clive Bell was unfaithful, Vanessa began an affair with Fry, and Fry began a lifelong debate with Virginia about the visual and verbal arts.

In the summer of 1911, Leonard Woolf returned from the East. After he resigned from the colonial service, Leonard and Virginia married in August 1912. She continued to work on her first novel; he wrote the anticolonialist novel *The Village in the Jungle* (1913) and *The Wise Virgins* (1914), a Bloomsbury exposé. Then he became a political writer and an advocate for peace and justice.

Between 1910 and 1915, Virginia's mental health was precarious. Nevertheless, she completely recast *Melymbrosia* as *The Voyage Out* in 1913. She based many of her novel's characters on real-life prototypes: Lytton Strachey, Leslie Stephen, her half brother George Duckworth, Clive and Vanessa Bell, and herself. Rachel Vinrace, the novel's central character, is a sheltered young woman who, on an excursion to South America, is introduced to freedom and sexuality (though from the novel's inception she was to die before marrying). Woolf first made Terence, Rachel's suitor, rather Clive-like; as she revised, Terence became a more sensitive, Leonard-like character. After an excursion up the Amazon, Rachel contracts a terrible illness that plunges her into delirium and then death. As possible causes for this disaster, Woolf's characters suggest everything from poorly washed vegetables to jungle disease to a malevolent universe, but the book endorses no explanation. That indeterminacy, at odds with the certainties of the Victorian era, is echoed in descriptions that distort perception: while the narrative often describes people, buildings, and natural objects as featureless forms, Rachel, in dreams and then delirium, journeys into surrealistic worlds. Rachel's voyage into the unknown began Woolf's voyage beyond the conventions of realism.

Woolf's manic-depressive worries (that she was a failure as a writer and a woman, that she was despised by Vanessa and unloved by Leonard) provoked a suicide attempt in September 1913. Publication of *The Voyage Out* was delayed until early 1915; then, that April, she sank into a distressed state in which she was often delirious. Later that year she overcame the "vile imaginations" that had threatened her sanity. She kept the demons of mania and depression mostly at bay for the rest of her life.

In 1917, the Woolfs bought a printing press and founded the Hogarth Press, named for Hogarth House, their home in the London suburbs. The Woolfs themselves (she was the compositor while he worked the press) published their own *Two Stories* in the summer of 1917. It consisted of Leonard's *Three Jews* and Virginia's *The Mark on the Wall*, the latter about contemplation itself.

Since 1910, Virginia had kept (sometimes with Vanessa) a country house in Sussex, and in 1916 Vanessa settled into a Sussex farmhouse called Charleston. She had ended her affair with Fry to take up with the painter Duncan Grant, who moved to Charleston with Vanessa and her children, Julian and Quentin Bell; a daughter, Angelica, would be born to Vanessa and Grant at the end of 1918. Charleston soon became an extravagantly decorated, unorthodox retreat for artists and writers, especially Clive Bell, who continued on friendly terms with Vanessa, and Fry, Vanessa's lifelong devotee.

Virginia had kept a diary, off and on, since 1897. In 1919 she envisioned "the shadow of some kind of form which a diary might attain to," organized not by a mechanical recording of events but by the interplay between the objective and the subjective. Her diary, as she wrote in 1924, would reveal people as "splinters & mosaics; not, as they used to hold, immaculate, monolithic, consistent wholes." Such terms later inspired critical distinctions, based on anatomy and culture, between the feminine and the masculine, the feminine being a varied but all-embracing way of experiencing the world and the masculine a monolithic or linear way. Critics using these distinctions have credited Woolf with evolving a distinctly feminine diary form, one that explores, with perception, honesty, and humor, her own ever-changing, mosaic self.

Proving that she could master the traditional form of the novel before breaking it, she plotted her next novel in two romantic triangles, with its protagonist Katharine in both. *Night and Day* (1919) answers Leonard's *The Wise Virgins*, in which he had his Leonard-like protagonist lose the Virginia-like beloved and end up in a conventional marriage. In *Night and Day*, the Leonard-like Ralph learns to value Katharine for herself, not as some superior being. And Katharine overcomes (as Virginia had) class and familial prejudices to marry the good and intelligent Ralph. This novel focuses on the very sort of details that Woolf had deleted from *The Voyage Out*: credible dialogue, realistic descriptions of early 20th-century settings, and investigations of issues such as class, politics, and suffrage.

Woolf was writing nearly a review a week for the *Times*

Literary Supplement in 1918. Her essay "Modern Novels" (1919; revised in 1925 as "Modern Fiction") attacked the "materialists" who wrote about superficial rather than spiritual or "luminous" experiences. The Woolfs also printed by hand, with Vanessa Bell's illustrations, Virginia's *Kew Gardens* (1919), a story organized, like a Post-Impressionistic painting, by pattern. With the Hogarth Press's emergence as a major publishing house, the Woolfs gradually ceased being their own printers.

In 1919, they bought a cottage in Rodmell village called Monk's House, which looked out over the Sussex Downs and the meadows where the River Ouse wound down to the English Channel. Virginia could walk or bicycle to visit Vanessa, her children, and a changing cast of guests at the bohemian Charleston and then retreat to Monk's House to write. She envisioned a new book that would apply the theories of "Modern Novels" and the achievements of her short stories to the novel form. In early 1920, a group of friends, evolved from the early Bloomsbury group, began a "Memoir Club," which met to read irreverent passages from their autobiographies. Her second presentation was an exposé of Victorian hypocrisy, especially that of George Duckworth, who masked inappropriate, unwanted caresses as affection honoring their mother's memory.

In 1921, Woolf's minimally plotted short fictions were gathered in *Monday or Tuesday*. Meanwhile, typesetting having heightened her sense of visual layout, she began a new novel written in blocks to be surrounded by white spaces. In "On Re Reading Novels" (1922), Woolf argued that the novel was not so much a form but an "emotion which you feel." In *Jacob's Room* (1922) she achieved such emotion, transforming personal grief over the death of Thoby Stephen into a "spiritual shape." Though she takes Jacob from childhood to his early death in war, she leaves out plot, conflict, even character. The emptiness of Jacob's

This 1902 portrait of Virginia Woolf captures the writer's likeness at age 20.

room and the irrelevance of his belongings convey in their minimalism the profound emptiness of loss. Though *Jacob's Room* is an antiwar novel, Woolf feared that she had ventured too far beyond representation. She vowed to "push on," as she wrote Clive Bell, to graft such experimental techniques onto more-substantial characters.

MAJOR PERIOD

At the beginning of 1924, the Woolfs moved their city residence from the suburbs back to Bloomsbury, where they were less isolated from London society. Soon the aristocratic Vita Sackville-West began to court Virginia, a relationship that would blossom into a lesbian affair. Having already written a story about a Mrs. Dalloway, Woolf thought of a foiling device that would pair that highly sensitive woman with a shell-shocked war victim, a Mr. Smith, so that "the sane and the insane" would exist "side by side." Her aim was to "tunnel" into these two characters until Clarissa Dalloway's affirmations meet Septimus Smith's negations. Also in 1924 Woolf gave a talk at Cambridge called "Character in Fiction," revised later that year as the Hogarth Press pamphlet *Mr. Bennett and Mrs. Brown*. In it she celebrated the breakdown in patriarchal values that had occurred "in or about December, 1910"—during Fry's exhibit "Manet and the Post-Impressionists"—and she attacked "materialist" novelists for omitting the essence of character.

In *Mrs. Dalloway* (1925), the boorish doctors presume to understand personality, but its essence evades them. This novel is as patterned as a Post-Impressionist painting but is also so accurately representational that the reader can trace Clarissa's and Septimus's movements through the streets of London on a single day in June 1923. At the end of the day, Clarissa gives a grand party and Septimus dies by suicide. Their lives come together when the doctor who was treating (or, rather, mistreating) Septimus arrives at Clarissa's party with news of the death. The main characters are connected by motifs and, finally, by Clarissa's intuiting why Septimus threw his life away.

Woolf wished to build on her achievement in *Mrs. Dalloway* by merging the novelistic and elegiac forms. As an elegy, *To the Lighthouse*—published on May 5, 1927, the 32nd anniversary of Julia Stephen's death—evoked childhood summers at Talland House. As a novel, it broke narrative continuity into a tripartite structure. The first section, "The Window," begins as Mrs. Ramsay and James, her youngest son—like Julia and Adrian Stephen—sit in the French window of the Ramsays' summer home while a houseguest named Lily Briscoe paints them and James begs to go to a nearby lighthouse. Mr. Ramsay, like Leslie Stephen, sees poetry as didacticism, conversation as winning points, and life as a tally of accomplishments. He uses logic to deflate hopes for a trip to the lighthouse, but he needs sympathy from his wife. She is more attuned to emotions than reason. In the climactic dinner-party scene, she inspires such harmony and composure that the moment "partook, she felt, . . . of eternity."

The novel's middle "Time Passes" section focuses on the empty house during a 10-year hiatus and the last-minute housecleaning for the returning Ramsays. Woolf describes the progress of weeds, mold, dust, and gusts of wind, but she merely announces such major events as the deaths of Mrs. Ramsay and a son and daughter. In the novel's third section, "The Lighthouse," Woolf brings Mr. Ramsay, his youngest children (James and Cam), Lily Briscoe, and others from "The Window" back to the house. As Mr. Ramsay and the now-teenage children reach the lighthouse and achieve a moment of reconciliation, Lily completes her painting.

To the Lighthouse melds into its structure questions about creativity and the nature and function of art. Lily argues effectively for nonrepresentational but emotive art, and her painting (in which mother and child are reduced to two shapes with a line between them) echoes the abstract structure of Woolf's profoundly elegiac novel.

In two 1927 essays, "The Art of Fiction" and "The New Biography," she wrote that fiction writers should be less concerned with naive notions of reality and more with language and design. However restricted by fact, she argued, biographers should yoke truth with imagination, "granite-like solidity" with "rainbow-like intangibility." Their relationship having cooled by 1927, Woolf sought to reclaim Sackville-West through a "biography" that would include Sackville family history.

Woolf solved biographical, historical, and personal dilemmas with the story of Orlando, who lives from Elizabethan times through the entire 18th century; he then becomes female, experiences debilitating gender constraints, and lives into the 20th century. Orlando begins writing poetry during the Renaissance, using history and mythology as models, and over the ensuing centuries returns to the poem "The Oak Tree," revising it according to shifting poetic conventions. Woolf herself writes in mock-heroic imitation of biographical styles that change over the same period of time. Thus, *Orlando: A Biography* (1928) exposes the artificiality of both gender and genre prescriptions. However fantastic, *Orlando* also argues for a novelistic approach to biography.

In 1921, John Maynard Keynes had told Woolf that her memoir "on George," presented to the Memoir Club that year or a year earlier, represented her best writing. Afterward she was increasingly angered by masculine condescension to female talent. In *A Room of One's Own* (1929), Woolf blamed women's absence from history not on their lack of brains and talent but on their poverty. For her 1931 talk "Professions for Women," Woolf studied the history of women's education and employment and argued that unequal opportunities for women negatively affect all of society. She urged women to destroy the "angel in the house," a reference to Coventry Patmore's poem of that title, the quintessential Victorian paean to women who sacrifice themselves to men.

Having praised a 1930 exhibit of Vanessa Bell's paintings for their wordlessness, Woolf planned a mystical novel that would be similarly impersonal and abstract. In *The Waves* (1931), poetic interludes describe the sea and sky from dawn to dusk. Between the interludes, the voices of six named characters appear in sections that move from their childhood to old age. In the middle section, when the six friends meet at a farewell dinner for another friend leaving for India, the single flower at the center of the dinner table becomes a "seven-sided flower . . . a whole flower to which every eye brings its own contribution." *The Waves* offers a six-sided shape that illustrates how each individual experiences events—including their friend's death—uniquely. Bernard, the writer in the group, narrates the final section, defying death and a world "without a self." Unique though they are (and their prototypes can be identified in the Bloomsbury group), the characters become one, just as the sea and sky become indistinguishable in the interludes. This oneness with all creation was the primal experience Woolf had felt as a child in Cornwall. In this her most experimental novel, she achieved its poetic equivalent.

Through *To the Lighthouse* and *The Waves*, Woolf became, with James Joyce and William Faulkner, one of the three major English-language Modernist experimenters in stream-of-consciousness writing.

Late Work

From her earliest days, Woolf had framed experience in terms of oppositions, even while she longed for a holistic state beyond binary divisions. The "perpetual marriage of granite and rainbow" Woolf described in her essay "The New Biography" typified her approach during the 1930s to individual works and to a balance between writing works of fact and of imagination. Even before finishing *The Waves*, she began compiling a scrapbook of clippings illustrating the horrors of war, the threat of fascism, and the oppression of women. The discrimination against women that Woolf had discussed in *A Room of One's Own* and "Professions for Women" inspired her to plan a book that would trace the story of a fictional family named Pargiter and explain the social conditions affecting family members over a period of time. In *The Pargiters: A Novel-Essay*, she would alternate between sections of fiction and sections of fact. For the fictional historical narrative, she relied upon experiences of friends and family from the Victorian Age to the 1930s. For the essays, she researched that 50-year span of history. The task, however, of moving between fiction and fact was daunting.

Woolf took a holiday from *The Pargiters* to write a mock biography of Flush, the dog of poet Elizabeth Barrett Browning. Lytton Strachey having recently died, Woolf muted her spoof of his biographical method; nevertheless, *Flush* (1933) remains both a biographical satire and a lighthearted exploration of perception, in this case a dog's. In 1935, Woolf completed *Freshwater*, an absurdist drama based on the life of her great-aunt Julia Margaret Cameron. Featuring such other eminences as the poet Alfred, Lord Tennyson, and the painter George Frederick Watts, this riotous play satirizes high-minded Victorian notions of art.

Meanwhile, Woolf feared she would never finish *The Pargiters*. Alternating between types of prose was proving cumbersome, and the book was becoming too long. She solved this dilemma by jettisoning the essay sections, keeping the family narrative, and renaming her book *The Years*. She narrated 50 years of family history through the decline of class and patriarchal systems, the rise of feminism, and the threat of another war. Desperate to finish, Woolf lightened the book with poetic echoes of gestures, objects, colors, and sounds and with wholesale deletions, cutting epiphanies for Eleanor Pargiter and explicit references to women's bodies. The novel illustrates the damage done to women and society over the years by sexual repression, ignorance, and discrimination. Though (or perhaps because) Woolf's trimming muted the book's radicalism, *The Years* (1937) became a bestseller.

When Fry died in 1934, Virginia was distressed; Vanessa was devastated. Then in July 1937, Vanessa's elder son, Julian Bell, was killed in the Spanish Civil War while driving an ambulance for the Republican army. Vanessa was so disconsolate that Virginia put aside her writing for a time to try to comfort her sister. Privately a lament over Julian's death and publicly a diatribe against war, *Three Guineas* (1938) proposes answers to the question of how to prevent war. Woolf connected masculine symbols of authority with militarism and misogyny, an argument buttressed by notes from her clippings about aggression, fascism, and war.

Still distressed by the deaths of Roger Fry and Julian Bell, she determined to test her theories about experimental, novelistic biography in a life of Fry. As she acknowledged in "The Art of Biography" (1939), the recalcitrance of evidence brought her near despair over the possibility of writing an imaginative biography. Against the "grind" of finishing the Fry biography, Woolf wrote a verse play about the history of English literature.

Her next novel, *Pointz Hall* (later retitled *Between the Acts*), would include the play as a pageant performed by villagers and would convey the gentry's varied reactions to it. As another holiday from Fry's biography, Woolf returned to her own childhood with "A Sketch of the Past," a memoir about her mixed feelings toward her parents and her past and about memoir writing itself. (Here surfaced for the first time in writing a memory of the teenage Gerald Duckworth, her other half brother, touching her inappropriately when she was a girl of perhaps four or five.) Through last-minute borrowing from the letters between Fry and Vanessa, Woolf finished her biography. Though convinced that *Roger Fry* (1940) was more granite than rainbow, Virginia congratulated herself on at least giving back to Vanessa "her Roger."

Woolf's chief anodyne against Adolf Hitler, World War II, and her own despair was writing. During the bombing of London in 1940 and 1941, she worked on her memoir and *Between the Acts*. In her novel, war threatens art and humanity itself, and, in the interplay between the pageant—performed on a June day in 1939—and the audience, Woolf raises questions about perception and response. Despite *Between the Acts*'s affirmation of the value of art, Woolf worried that this novel was "too slight" and indeed that all writing was irrelevant when England seemed on the verge of invasion and civilization about to slide over a precipice. Facing such horrors, a depressed Woolf found herself unable to write. The demons of self-doubt that she had kept at bay for so long returned to haunt her. On March 28, 1941, fearing that she now lacked the resilience to battle them, she walked behind Monk's House and down to the River Ouse, put stones in her pockets, and drowned herself. *Between the Acts* was published posthumously later that year.

Assessment

Woolf's experiments with point of view confirm that as Bernard thinks in *The Waves*, "we are not single." Being neither single nor fixed, perception in her novels is fluid, as is the world she presents. While Joyce and Faulkner separate one character's interior monologues from another's, Woolf's narratives move between inner and outer and between characters without clear demarcations. Furthermore, she avoids the self-absorption of many of her contemporaries and implies a brutal society without the explicit details some of her contemporaries felt obligatory. Her nonlinear forms invite reading not for neat solutions but for an aesthetic resolution of "shivering fragments," as she wrote in 1908. While Woolf's fragmented style is distinctly Modernist, her indeterminacy anticipates a postmodern awareness of the evanescence of boundaries and categories.

Woolf's many essays about the art of writing and about reading itself today retain their appeal to a range of, in Samuel Johnson's words, "common" (unspecialized) readers. Woolf's collection of essays *The Common Reader* (1925) was followed by *The Common Reader: Second Series* (1932; also published as *The Second Common Reader*). She continued writing essays on reading and writing, women and history, and class and politics for the rest of her life. Many were collected after her death in volumes edited by Leonard Woolf.

Virginia Woolf wrote far more fiction than Joyce and far more nonfiction than either Joyce or Faulkner. Six volumes of diaries (including her early journals), six volumes of letters, and numerous volumes of collected essays show her deep engagement with major 20th-century issues. Though many of her essays began as reviews, written anonymously to deadlines for money, and many include imaginative settings and whimsical speculations, they are serious inquiries into reading and writing, the novel and the arts, perception and essence, war and peace, class and politics, privilege and discrimination, and the need to reform society.

Woolf's haunting language, her prescient insights into wide-ranging historical, political, feminist, and artistic issues, and her revisionist experiments with novelistic form during a remarkably productive career altered the course of Modernist and postmodernist letters.

COCO CHANEL
(b. Aug. 19, 1883, Saumur, France—d. Jan. 10, 1971, Paris)

The French fashion designer Coco Chanel ruled over Parisian haute couture for almost six decades. Her elegantly casual designs inspired women of fashion to abandon the complicated, uncomfortable clothes—such as petticoats and corsets—that were prevalent in 19th-century dress. Among her now-classic innovations were the Chanel suit, costume jewelry, and the "little black dress."

Gabrielle Bonheur Chanel was born into poverty in the French countryside; her mother died, and her father abandoned her to an orphanage. After a brief stint as a shopgirl and a failed attempt to become a café singer, Chanel engaged in liaisons with a series of wealthy men. In 1913, with financial assistance from one of these men, she opened a tiny millinery shop in Deauville, where she also sold simple sportswear, such as jersey sweaters. Within five years, her original use of jersey fabric to create a "poor girl" look had attracted the attention of influential wealthy women seeking relief from the prevalent corseted styles. Faithful to her maxim that "luxury must be comfortable, otherwise it is not luxury," Chanel's designs stressed simplicity and comfort and revolutionized the fashion industry.

By the late 1920s, the Chanel industries employed 3,500 people and included a couture house, a textile business, perfume laboratories, and a workshop for costume jewelry.

The financial basis of this empire was Chanel No. 5, the phenomenally successful perfume she introduced in 1922 with the help of Ernst Beaux, one of the most talented perfume creators in France. It has been said that the perfume got its name from the series of scents that Beaux created for Chanel to sample—she chose the fifth, a combination of jasmine and several other floral scents that was more complex and mysterious than the single-scented perfumes then on the market. That Chanel was the first major fashion designer to introduce a perfume and that she replaced the typical perfume packaging with a simple and sleek bottle also added to the scent's success. Unfortunately, her partnerships with businessmen Théophile Bader and Pierre Wertheimer, who promised to help her market her fragrance in exchange for a share of the profits, meant that she received only 10 percent of its royalties before World War II and only 2 percent afterward. Despite enacting a series of lawsuits, Chanel failed to regain control of her signature fragrance.

Chanel closed her couture house in 1939 with the outbreak of World War II but returned in 1954 to introduce her highly copied suit design: a collarless, braid-trimmed cardigan jacket with a graceful skirt. She also introduced bell-bottomed pants and other innovations, while always retaining a clean, classic look.

After her death in 1971, Chanel's couture house was led by a series of different designers. This situation stabilized in 1983, when Karl Lagerfeld became chief designer.

ELEANOR ROOSEVELT

(b. Oct. 11, 1884, New York, N.Y., U.S.—d. Nov. 7, 1962, New York City)

Eleanor Roosevelt was an American first lady (1933–45), the wife of Franklin D. Roosevelt, 32nd president of the United States, and a United Nations diplomat and humanitarian. She was, in her time, one of the world's most widely admired and powerful women.

Anna Eleanor Roosevelt was the daughter of Elliott and Anna Hall Roosevelt and the niece of Theodore Roosevelt, 26th president of the United States. She grew up in a wealthy family that attached great value to community service. Both her parents died before she was 10, and she and her surviving brother (another brother died when she was 9) were raised by relatives. The death of Eleanor's father, to whom she had been especially close, was very difficult for her.

At age 15, Eleanor enrolled at Allenswood, a girls' boarding school outside London, where she came under the influence of the French headmistress, Marie Souvestre. Souvestre's intellectual curiosity and her taste for travel and excellence—in everything but sports—awakened similar interests in Eleanor, who later described her three years there as the happiest time of her life. Reluctantly, she returned to New York in the summer of 1902 to prepare for her "coming out" into society that winter. Following family tradition, she devoted time to community service, including teaching in a settlement house on Manhattan's Lower East Side.

Early Life with Franklin

Soon after Eleanor returned to New York, Franklin Roosevelt, her distant cousin, began to court her, and they were married on March 17, 1905, in New York City. His taste for fun contrasted with her own seriousness, and she often commented on how he had to find companions in pleasure elsewhere. Between 1906 and 1916 Eleanor gave birth to six children, one of whom died in infancy.

After Franklin won a seat in the New York Senate in 1911, the family moved to Albany, where Eleanor was initiated into the job of political wife. When Franklin was appointed assistant secretary of the navy in 1913, the family moved to Washington, D.C., and Eleanor spent the next few years performing the social duties expected of an "official wife," including attending formal parties and making social calls in the homes of other government officials. For the most part, she found these occasions tedious.

With the entry of the United States into World War I in April 1917, Eleanor was able to resume her volunteer work. She visited wounded soldiers and worked for the Navy–Marine Corps Relief Society and in a Red Cross canteen. This work increased her sense of self-worth, and she wrote later, "I loved it . . . I simply ate it up."

In 1918, Eleanor discovered that Franklin had been having an affair with her social secretary, Lucy Mercer. It was one of the most traumatic events in her life, as she later told Joseph Lash, her friend and biographer. Mindful of his political career and fearing the loss of his mother's financial support, Franklin refused Eleanor's offer of a divorce and agreed to stop seeing Mercer. The Roosevelts' marriage settled into a routine in which both principals kept independent agendas while remaining respectful of and affectionate toward each other. But their relationship had ceased to be an intimate one. Later, Mercer and other glamorous, witty women continued to attract his attention and claim his time, and later in 1945 Mercer, by then the widow of Winthrop Rutherfurd, was with Franklin when he died at Warm Springs, Georgia.

Franklin ran unsuccessfully for vice president on the

Democratic ticket in 1920. At this time Eleanor's interest in politics increased, partly as a result of her decision to help in her husband's political career after he was stricken with poliomyelitis in 1921 and partly as a result of her desire to work for important causes. She joined the Women's Trade Union League and became active in the New York state Democratic Party. As a member of the Legislative Affairs Committee of the League of Women Voters, she began studying the Congressional Record and learned to evaluate voting records and debates.

When Franklin became governor of New York in 1929, Eleanor found an opportunity to combine the responsibilities of a political hostess with her own burgeoning career and personal independence. She continued to teach at Todhunter, a girls' school in Manhattan that she and two friends had purchased, making several trips a week back and forth between Albany and New York City.

In the White House

During her 12 years as first lady, the unprecedented breadth of Eleanor's activities and her advocacy of liberal causes made her nearly as controversial a figure as her husband. She instituted regular White House press conferences for women correspondents, and wire services that had not formerly employed women were forced to do so in order to have a representative present in case important news broke. In deference to the president's infirmity, she helped serve as his eyes and ears throughout the nation, embarking on extensive tours and reporting to him on conditions, programs, and public opinion. These unusual excursions were the butt of some criticism and "Eleanor jokes" by her opponents, but many people responded warmly to her compassionate interest in their welfare. Beginning in 1936, she also wrote a daily syndicated newspaper column,

Eleanor Roosevelt, shown here in 1932, expressed her humanitarian interests through her role as first lady.

"My Day."

A widely sought-after speaker at political meetings and at various institutions, she showed particular interest in child welfare, housing reform, and equal rights for women and racial minorities.

In 1939, when the Daughters of the American Revolution (DAR) refused to let Marian Anderson, an African American opera singer, perform in Constitution Hall, Eleanor resigned her membership in the DAR and arranged to hold the concert at the nearby Lincoln Memorial; the event turned into a massive outdoor celebration attended by 75,000 people. On another occasion, when local officials in Alabama insisted that seating at a public meeting be segregated by race, Eleanor carried a folding chair to all sessions and carefully placed it in the center aisle. Her defense of the rights of African Americans, youth, and the poor helped to bring groups into government that formerly had been alienated from the political process.

Later Years

After President Roosevelt's death in 1945, President Harry S. Truman appointed Eleanor a delegate to the United Nations (UN), where she served as chairman of the Commission on Human Rights (1946–51) and played a major role in the drafting and adoption of the Universal Declaration of Human Rights (1948). In the last decade of her life she continued to play an active part in the Democratic Party, working for the election of Democratic presidential nominee Adlai Stevenson in 1952 and 1956.

In 1961, President John F. Kennedy appointed her chair of his Commission on the Status of Women, and she continued with that work until shortly before her death. She had not initially favored the Equal Rights Amendment

(ERA), saying it would take from women the valuable protective legislation that they had fought to win and still needed, but she gradually embraced it.

An indefatigable traveler, Eleanor Roosevelt circled the globe several times, visiting scores of countries and meeting with most of the world's leaders. She continued to write books and articles, and the last of her "My Day" columns appeared just weeks before her death, from a rare form of tuberculosis, in 1962. She is buried at Hyde Park, her husband's family home on the Hudson River and the site of the Franklin D. Roosevelt Library. In many ways, it was her library too, since she had carved out such an important record as first lady, one against which all her successors would be judged.

KAREN HORNEY

(b. Sept. 16, 1885, Blankenese, near Hamburg, Ger.—d. Dec. 4, 1952, New York, N.Y., U.S.)

Departing from some of the basic principles of Sigmund Freud, the German-born American psychoanalyst Karen Horney proposed an environmental and social basis for the personality and its disorders.

Karen Danielsen married Oscar Horney, a lawyer, in 1909. She studied medicine at the universities of Freiburg, Göttingen, and Berlin, taking an MD degree from the last in 1911. After a period of medical practice, Karen Horney became interested in psychoanalysis. From 1913 to 1915 she studied and entered analysis with Karl Abraham, a close associate and disciple of Sigmund Freud. From 1915 to 1920, she engaged in clinical and outpatient psychiatric work in connection with Berlin hospitals, and in 1920 she joined the teaching staff of the newly founded Berlin Psychoanalytic Institute.

Although she adhered in the main to the outlines of

Freudian theory, Horney early began to disagree with Freud's view of female psychology, which he treated as an offshoot of male psychology. Unaffected by the worshipful awe that held many early Freudians to received dogma, she forthrightly rejected such notions as penis envy and other manifestations of male bias in psychoanalytic theory. She argued instead that the source of much female psychiatric disturbance is located in the very male-dominated culture that had produced Freudian theory. She introduced the concept of womb envy, suggesting that male envy of pregnancy, nursing, and motherhood—of women's primary role in creating and sustaining life—led men to claim their superiority in other fields.

Horney and her husband separated in 1926, and divorced in 1937. During this time, in 1932, she went to the United States to become associate director of the Institute for Psychoanalysis in Chicago. She moved to New York City in 1934 to return to private practice and teach at the New School for Social Research. There she produced her major theoretical works, *The Neurotic Personality of Our Time* (1937) and *New Ways in Psychoanalysis* (1939), in which she argued that environmental and social conditions, rather than the instinctual or biological drives described by Freud, determine much of individual personality and are the chief causes of neuroses and personality disorders. In particular, Horney objected to Freud's concepts of the libido, the death instinct, and the Oedipus complex, which she thought could be more adequately explained by cultural and social conditions. She believed that a primary condition responsible for the later development of neurosis was the infant's experience of basic anxiety, in which the child felt "isolated and helpless in a potentially hostile world." The various strategies the child adopts to cope with this anxiety can eventually become persistent and irrational needs that cause both neurosis and personality disorder.

Many of Horney's ideas, rooted as they were in her wide clinical experience, were translated into a new approach to psychoanalytic therapy. She sought to help patients identify the specific cause of present anxieties, thinking that it was just as important to the goals of psychoanalysis to deal with real-life, present-day problems as it was to reconstruct childhood emotional states and fantasies. In many cases, she suggested that the patient could even learn to psychoanalyze himself.

Her refusal to adhere to strict Freudian theory caused Horney's expulsion from the New York Psychoanalytic Institute in 1941, which left her free to organize a new group, the Association for the Advancement of Psychoanalysis, and its affiliated teaching center, the American Institute for Psychoanalysis. Horney founded the association's *American Journal of Psychoanalysis* and served as its editor until her death in 1952. She also continued to write, further expounding her views that neuroses were caused by disturbances in interpersonal relationships in *Our Inner Conflicts* (1945) and *Neurosis and Human Growth* (1950). The Karen Horney Foundation was established in New York the year of her death and gave rise in 1955 to the Karen Horney Clinic. Horney's analysis of the causes and the dynamics of neurosis and her revision of Freud's theory of personality have remained influential. Her ideas on female psychosexual development were given particular attention after *Feminine Psychology*, a collection of her early papers on the subject, was published in 1967.

MARTHA GRAHAM

(b. May 11, 1894, Allegheny county, Pa., U.S.—d. April 1, 1991, New York, N.Y.)

Martha Graham was an influential American dancer, teacher, and choreographer of modern dance, whose ballets and other works were intended to "reveal the inner man." Over 50-plus years she created more than 180 works, from solos to large-scale works, in most of which she herself danced. She gave modern dance new depth as a vehicle for the intense and forceful expression of primal emotions.

Early Life and Works

Graham was one of three daughters of a physician who was particularly interested in the bodily expression of human behavior. After some time in the South, her family settled in 1909 in Santa Barbara, California, where she discovered the rhythm of the sea and became acquainted with Oriental art, influences that were to be evident in her choreography throughout her career.

Graham's professional career began in 1916 at Denishawn, the school and dance company founded in Los Angeles by Ruth St. Denis and Ted Shawn, where as a teenager she was introduced to a repertory and curriculum that, for the first time in the United States, explored the world's dances—folk, classical, experimental, Oriental, and American Indian. She was entranced by the religious mysticism of St. Denis, but Shawn was her major teacher; he discovered sources of dramatic power within her and then channeled them into an Aztec ballet, *Xochitl*. The dance was a tremendous success both in vaudeville and in concert performance and made her a Denishawn star.

Graham remained with Denishawn until 1923, and although she ultimately rebelled violently against its eclecticism, she later mirrored in her own works the Orientalism that pervaded the school. She left Denishawn to become a featured dancer in the Greenwich Village Follies revue, where she remained for two years. In 1924 she went to the Eastman School of Music in Rochester,

New York, to teach and to experiment.

Graham made her New York City debut as an independent artist in 1926. Though some of the fruits of her experiments were discernible from the first, a good many of her dances, such as *Three Gopi Maidens* and *Danse Languide*, echoed her Denishawn past. The critics found her to be graceful and lyrical. All of that changed with her 1927 concert, and for the next decade and more, the startlingly original dances she performed were to be referred to as ugly, stark, and obscure. The exotic costumes and rich staging of Denishawn were in the past. Among the dances of her 1927 program was *Revolt*, probably the first dance of protest and social comment staged in the United States, which was set to the avant-garde music of Arthur Honegger. The audience was not impressed; dancers and theatergoers, famous and unknown, ridiculed her. Graham herself later referred to this decade as "my period of long woolens," a reference to the plain jersey dress that she wore in many of her dances.

A strong and continuing influence in her life was Louis Horst, musical director at Denishawn, who had left the school two years after Graham. He became her musical director, often composing pieces for her during her first two decades of independence; they remained close until his death in 1964. Among his most noted scores for her were those for the now historic *Frontier* (1935), a solo dance, and *Primitive Mysteries*, written for Graham and a company of female dancers.

Frontier initiated the use of decor in Graham's repertoire and marked the beginning of a long and distinguished collaboration with the noted Japanese-American sculptor Isamu Noguchi, under whose influence she developed one of her most singular stage innovations, the use of sculpture, or three-dimensional set pieces, instead of flats and drops.

MATURITY

For Martha Graham, the dance, like the spoken drama, can explore the spiritual and emotional essence of human beings. Thus, the choreography of *Frontier* symbolized the frontier woman's achievement of mastery over an uncharted domain. In *Night Journey* (1948), a work about the Greek legendary figure Jocasta, the whole dance-drama takes place in the instant when Jocasta learns that she has mated with Oedipus, her own son, and has borne him children. The work treats Jocasta rather than Oedipus as the tragic victim, and shows her reliving the events of her life and seeking justification for her actions. In *Letter to the World* (1940), a work about Emily Dickinson, several characters are used to portray different aspects of the poet's personality.

For more than 10 years, Graham's dance company consisted solely of women, but her themes were beginning to call for men as well. She engaged Erick Hawkins, a ballet dancer, to join her company, and he appeared with her in a major work, *American Document* (1938). Though she and Hawkins were married in 1948, the marriage did not last.

In a career spanning more than half a century, Graham created a succession of dances, ranging from solos to large-scale creations of full-program length such as *Clytemnestra* (1958). For her themes she almost always turned to human conflicts and emotions. The settings and the eras vary, but her great gallery of danced portraits never failed to explore the inner emotional life of their characters. She created some dances from American frontier life, the most famous of which is *Appalachian Spring* (1944), with its score by Aaron Copland. Another source was Greek legend, the dances rooted in Classical Greek dramas, stories, and myths. *Cave of the Heart* (1946), based on the figure of

Medea, with music by Samuel Barber, was not a dance version of the legend but rather an exposure of the Medea latent in every woman who, out of consuming jealousy, not only destroys those she loves but herself as well.

Later works by Graham also borrowed from Greek legend, including *Errand into the Maze* (1947), an investigation of hidden fears presented through the symbols of the Minotaur and the labyrinth; *Alcestis* (1960); *Phaedra* (1962); and *Circe* (1963). Biblical themes and religious figures also inspired her: *Seraphic Dialogue* (1955; Joan of Arc), *Embattled Garden* (1958; referring to the Garden of Eden), and *Legend of Judith* (1962) and such fanciful abstractions as *Diversion of Angels* (1948) or *Acrobats of God* (1960). Her later works include *The Witch of Endor* (1965), *Cortege of Eagles* (1967), *The Archaic Hours* (1969), *Mendicants of Evening* (1973), *Lucifer* (1975), *The Owl and the Pussycat* (1978), and *Frescoes* (1980). In the early 1980s she created neoclassical dances, beginning with *Acts of Light* (1981). In 1970 she announced her retirement as a dancer, but she continued to create dances and to teach.

Assessment

Martha Graham created a dance technique that became the first significant alternative to the idiom of classical ballet. As the dancer Alma Guillermoprieto has pointed out, Graham was "the first creator of modern dance to devise a truly universal dance technique out of the movements she developed in her choreography." Her dance language was intended to express shared human emotions and experiences, rather than merely provide decorative displays of graceful movements. The dances were also intended to evoke a visceral response in the audience rather than be comprehended in primarily linear or pictorial terms. Many of her dances feature forceful, angular movements originating in spasms of muscular contraction and release centered in the dancer's pelvis. These expressive contractions help generate the strong sexual tension that is a feature of so many of Graham's works. The resulting dance vocabulary is startlingly unlike that of classical ballet in its jagged and angular lines, and its dislocations and distortions that express intensely felt human emotion. Her technique is the most highly developed body-training method in the entire field of modern dance, requiring both unrelenting discipline and prodigious virtuosity.

Throughout most of her career, Graham maintained a position as the foremost figure in American modern dance. She instructed, or guided, generations of modern dance teachers both in the United States and abroad. She strongly influenced succeeding generations of modern dancers, ballet choreographers, stagers of musicals and operas, and creators of dance-dramas. From the "long woolens" of the 1920s, Graham moved to some of the most opulent productions to be found in modern dance, with an accent on sculptured pieces and brilliant costumes and properties. She was the recipient of many awards and honors, including the Medal of Freedom, the highest civilian award in the United States. In 1973, she published *The Notebooks of Martha Graham*.

SOONG MEI-LING

(b. March 5, 1897, Shanghai, China—d. Oct. 23, 2003, New York, N.Y., U.S.)

Soong Mei-ling (Soong also spelled Sung, Mei-ling also spelled Mayling) was a notable Chinese political figure and second wife of the Nationalist Chinese president Chiang Kai-shek. She is also called Madame Chiang Kai-shek. Her family was successful, prosperous, and

Soong Mei-ling gave a special radio broadcast to thank the American people for their support of China during the Sino-Japanese War (1937–45).

well-connected: her sister Soong Ch'ing-ling (Song Qingling) was the wife of Sun Yat-sen, and her brother T. V. Soong was a prominent industrialist and official of the Nationalist Chinese government.

Soong Mei-ling was educated in the United States from 1908 to 1917, when she graduated from Wellesley College, and was thoroughly Americanized. In 1927, she married Chiang Kai-shek, and she helped introduce him to Western culture and ideas and worked to publicize his cause in the West. With her husband, she launched in 1934 the New Life Movement, a program that sought to halt the spread of communism by teaching traditional Chinese values. In 1936, Chiang Kai-shek was taken captive by Chang Hsüeh-liang, a warlord who believed the Nationalist government should stop fighting China's communists and instead concentrate on resisting Japanese aggression; Soong Mei-ling played a major role in the negotiations that led to his release.

During World War II, she wrote many articles on China for American journals, and in 1943, during a visit to the United States, she became the first Chinese and only the second woman to address a joint session of the U.S. Congress, where she sought increased support for China in its war against Japan. Her efforts resulted in much financial aid, and she so impressed the American public that until 1967 her name appeared annually on the U.S. list of the 10 most admired women in the world.

In the mid-1940s, civil war broke out in China as Nationalists and communists battled for control of the country. Chiang Kai-shek's forces were defeated in 1949, and Soong Mei-ling and her family moved to Taiwan, where her husband established his government. Still highly influential, she continued to seek support from the United States, and her efforts helped sway the U.S. government's policy toward China and Taiwan. After Chiang Kai-shek's death in 1975, Soong Mei-ling moved to New

York, where she lived in semi-seclusion. Following the death in 1988 of Chiang Ching-kuo, Chiang Kai-shek's son from his first marriage and the president of Taiwan, she briefly became involved in Taiwanese politics, but by that time her influence had greatly diminished. Her published works include *This Is Our China* (1940), *The Sure Victory* (1955), and two volumes of selected speeches.

AMELIA EARHART

(b. July 24, 1897, Atchison, Kan., U.S.—disappeared July 2, 1937, near Howland Island, central Pacific Ocean)

One of the world's most celebrated aviators, Amelia Earhart was the first woman to fly alone over the Atlantic Ocean.

Amelia Mary Earhart moved often with her family and completed high school in Chicago in 1916. She worked as a military nurse in Canada during World War I and as a social worker at Denison House in Boston after the war. She learned to fly (against her family's wishes) in 1920–21 and in 1922 bought her first plane, a Kinner Canary. On June 17–18, 1928, she became the first woman to fly across the Atlantic, although she was only a passenger in a plane flown by Wilmer Stutz and Louis Gordon. The same year, her reflections on that flight were published as *20 Hrs., 40 Min.* She married the publisher George Palmer Putnam in 1931 but continued her career under her maiden name.

Determined to justify the renown that her 1928 crossing had brought her, Earhart crossed the Atlantic alone on May 20–21, 1932. Her flight in her Lockheed Vega from Newfoundland to Ireland was completed in the record time of 14 hours 56 minutes. After that flight, she wrote *The Fun of It* (1932). This soon led to a series of flights across the United States and drew her into the movement that

Amelia Earhart fell in love with flying in 1920 and became a pioneer of aviation soon after.

encouraged the development of commercial aviation. She also took an active part in efforts to open aviation to women and end male domination in the new field.

In January 1935, she made a solo flight from Hawaii to California, a longer distance than that from the United States to Europe. Earhart was the first person to fly that hazardous route successfully; all previous attempts had ended in disaster. She set out in 1937 to fly around the world, with Fred Noonan as her navigator, in a twin-engine Lockheed Electra. After completing more than two-thirds of the distance, her plane vanished in the central Pacific near the International Date Line. Although her mysterious disappearance has since raised many questions and much speculation about the events surrounding it, the facts remain largely unknown.

IRÈNE JOLIOT-CURIE
(b. Sept. 12, 1897, Paris, France—d. March 17, 1956, Paris)

The French physical chemist Irène Joliot-Curie was awarded, with her husband, the 1935 Nobel Prize for Chemistry for the discovery of new radioactive isotopes prepared artificially. She was the daughter of Nobel Prize winners Pierre and Marie Curie.

Irène Curie from 1912 to 1914 prepared for her *baccalauréat* at the Collège Sévigné and in 1918 became her mother's assistant at the Institut du Radium of the University of Paris. In 1925, she presented her doctoral thesis on the alpha rays of polonium. In the same year she met Frédéric Joliot in her mother's laboratory; they were married the following year (on October 9, 1926). She was to find in him a mate who shared her interest in science, sports, humanism, and the arts. He learned laboratory techniques under Irène's guidance, and beginning in 1928 they signed their scientific work jointly.

In the course of their researches, they bombarded boron, aluminum, and magnesium with alpha particles; and they obtained radioactive isotopes of elements not ordinarily radioactive, namely, nitrogen, phosphorus, and aluminum. These discoveries revealed the possibility of using artificially produced radioactive isotopes to follow chemical changes and physiological processes, and such applications were soon successful; the absorption of radioiodine by the thyroid gland was detected, and the course of radiophosphorus (in the form of phosphates) was traced in the metabolism of the organism. The production of these unstable atomic nuclei afforded further means for the observation of changes in the atom as these nuclei broke down. The Joliot-Curies observed also the production of neutrons and positive electrons in the changes that they studied; and their discovery of artificial radioactive isotopes constituted an important step toward the solution of the problem of releasing the energy of the atom, since the method of Enrico Fermi, using neutrons instead of alpha particles for the bombardments which led to the fission of uranium, was an extension of the method developed by the Joliot-Curies for producing radioelements artificially.

In 1935, Frédéric and Irène Joliot-Curie were awarded the Nobel Prize for Chemistry for the synthesis of new radioactive isotopes. The Joliot-Curies then moved into a home at the edge of the Parc de Sceaux. They left it only for visits to their house in Brittany at Pointe de l'Arcouest, where university families had been meeting together since the time of Marie Curie.

In 1937, Frédéric having been appointed professor at the Collège de France, Irène then devoted her time largely to the upbringing of their children, Hélène and Pierre. But both she and Frédéric had a lofty idea of their human and social responsibilities. They had joined the Socialist

Party in 1934 and the Comité de Vigilance des Intellectuels Antifascistes (Vigilance Committee of Anti-Fascist Intellectuals) in 1935. They also took a stand in 1936 on the side of Republican Spain. Irène was one of three women to participate in the Popular Front government of 1936. As undersecretary of state for scientific research, she helped to lay the foundations, with Jean Perrin, for what would later become the Centre National de la Recherche Scientifique (National Center for Scientific Research).

Anxiety resulting from the rise of Nazism and the awareness of the dangers that could result from the application of chain reactions led them to cease publication. On October 30, 1939, they recorded the principle of nuclear reactors in a sealed envelope, which they deposited at the Académie des Sciences; it remained secret until 1949. Frédéric chose to remain in occupied France with his family and to make certain that the Germans who came into his laboratory could not use his work or his equipment, whose removal to Germany he prevented. The Joliot-Curies continued their research in biology.

In May 1944, Irène and their children took refuge in Switzerland, while Frédéric remained in Paris under an assumed name. After 1945, when General Charles de Gaulle tapped Frédéric for his atomic expertise, Irène devoted her scientific experience and her abilities as an administrator to the acquisition of raw materials, the prospecting for uranium, and the construction of detection installations. In 1946, she was also appointed director of the Institut du Radium. After 1950, the Joliot-Curies devoted themselves to laboratory work, to teaching, and to various peace movements.

During the 1950s, following several operations, Irène's health began to decline. In 1955, Irène drew up plans for the new nuclear physics laboratories at the Université d'Orsay, south of Paris, where teams of scientists could work with large particle accelerators under conditions less cramped than in the Parisian laboratories. Early in 1956, she was sent into the mountains to recuperate, but her condition did not improve. Wasted away by leukemia as her mother had been, she again entered the Curie Hospital, where she died in 1956.

GOLDA MEIR
(b. May 3, 1898, Kiev [Ukraine]—d. Dec. 8, 1978, Jerusalem, Israel)

Golda Meir was one of the founders of the State of Israel and its fourth prime minister (1969–74).

Born Goldie Mabovitch, Meir and her family immigrated to Milwaukee, Wisconsin, in 1906. She attended the Milwaukee Normal School (now the University of Wisconsin-Milwaukee) and later became a leader in the Milwaukee Labor Zionist Party. In 1921, she and her husband, Morris Myerson, emigrated to Palestine and joined the Merhavya kibbutz. She became the kibbutz's representative to the Histadrut (General Federation of Labor), the secretary of that organization's Women's Labor Council (1928–32), and a member of its executive committee (1934 until World War II).

During the war, Meir emerged as a forceful spokesperson for the Zionist cause in negotiating with the British mandatory authorities. In 1946, when the British arrested and detained many Jewish activists, including Moshe Sharett, head of the Political Department of the Jewish Agency, she provisionally replaced him and worked for the release of her comrades and the many Jewish war refugees who had violated British immigration regulations by settling in Palestine. Upon his release, Sharett took up diplomatic duties, and Meir officially took over his former position. She personally attempted to dissuade King

Golda Meir became the first female prime minister of Israel in 1969.

Abdullah of Jordan from joining the invasion of Israel decided on by other Arab states.

On May 14, 1948, Meir was a signatory of Israel's independence declaration and that year was appointed minister to Moscow. She was elected to the Knesset (Israeli parliament) in 1949 and served in that body until 1974. As minister of labor (1949–56), she carried out major programs of housing and road construction and vigorously supported the policy of unrestricted Jewish immigration to Israel. Appointed foreign minister in 1956, she Hebraized her name to Golda Meir. She promoted the Israeli policy of assistance to the new African states aimed at enhancing diplomatic support among uncommitted nations. Shortly after retiring from the Foreign Ministry in January 1966, she became secretary general of the Mapai Party and supported Prime Minister Levi Eshkol in intraparty conflicts. After Israel's victory in the Six-Day War (June 1967) against Egypt, Jordan, and Syria, she helped merge Mapai with two dissident parties into the Israel Labor Party.

Upon Eshkol's death on February 26, 1969, Meir, the compromise candidate, became prime minister. She maintained the coalition government that had emerged in June 1967. Meir pressed for a peace settlement in the Middle East by diplomatic means. She traveled widely, her meetings including those with Nicolae Ceaușescu in Romania (1972) and Pope Paul VI at the Vatican (1973). Also in 1973, Meir's government was host to Willy Brandt, chancellor of West Germany.

Her efforts at forging a peace with the Arab states were halted by the outbreak in October 1973 of the fourth Arab–Israeli war, called the Yom Kippur War. Israel's lack of readiness for the war stunned the nation, and Meir formed a new coalition government only with great difficulty in March 1974 and resigned her post as prime minister on

April 10. She remained in power as head of a caretaker government until a new one was formed in June. Although in retirement thereafter, she remained an important political figure. Upon her death, it was revealed that she had had leukemia for 12 years. Her autobiography, *My Life*, was published in 1975.

MARLENE DIETRICH

(b. Dec. 27, 1901, Schöneberg (now in Berlin), Germany—d. May 6, 1992, Paris, France)

The German American motion-picture actress Marlene Dietrich, one of the world's most glamorous film stars, was noted for her beauty, voice, aura of sophistication, and languid sensuality.

Dietrich was born Marie Magdalene Dietrich. Her father, Ludwig Dietrich, a Royal Prussian police officer, died when she was very young, and her mother remarried a cavalry officer, Edouard von Losch. Marlene, who as a girl adopted the compressed form of her first and middle names, studied at a private school and learned both English and French by age 12. As a teenager she studied to be a concert violinist, but her initiation into the nightlife of Weimar Berlin—with its cabarets and notorious demimonde—made the life of a classical musician unappealing to her. She pretended to have injured her wrist and was forced to seek other jobs acting and modeling to help make ends meet.

In 1921, Dietrich enrolled in Max Reinhardt's Deutsche Theaterschule, and she eventually joined Reinhardt's theater company. In 1923, she attracted the attention of Rudolf Sieber, a casting director at UFA film studios, who began casting her in small film roles. She and Sieber married the following year, and after the birth of their daughter, Maria, Dietrich returned to work on the stage and in films.

Although they did not divorce for decades, the couple separated in 1929.

That same year, director Josef von Sternberg first laid eyes on Dietrich and cast her as Lola-Lola, the sultry and world-weary female lead in *Der blaue Engel* (1930; *The Blue Angel*), Germany's first talking film. The film's success catapulted Dietrich to stardom. Von Sternberg took her to the United States and signed her with Paramount Pictures. With von Sternberg's help, Dietrich began to develop her legend by cultivating a femme fatale film persona in several von Sternberg vehicles that followed—*Morocco* (1930), *Dishonored* (1931), *Shanghai Express* (1932), *Blonde Venus* (1932), *The Scarlet Empress* (1934), and *The Devil Is a Woman* (1935). Dietrich showed a lighter side in *Desire* (1936), directed by Frank Borzage, and *Destry Rides Again* (1939).

During the Third Reich and despite Adolf Hitler's personal requests, Dietrich refused to work in Germany, and her films were temporarily banned there. Renouncing Nazism ("Hitler is an idiot," she stated in one wartime interview), Dietrich was branded a traitor in Germany; she was spat upon by Nazi supporters carrying banners that read "Go home Marlene" during her visit to Berlin in 1960. (In 2001, on the 100th anniversary of her birth, the city issued a formal apology for the incident.) Having become a U.S. citizen in 1937, she made more than 500 personal appearances before Allied troops from 1943 to 1946. She later said, "America took me into her bosom when I no longer had a native country worthy of the name, but in my heart I am German—German in my soul."

After the war, Dietrich continued to make successful films, such as *A Foreign Affair* (1948), *The Monte Carlo Story* (1956), *Witness for the Prosecution* (1957), *Touch of Evil* (1958), and *Judgment at Nuremberg* (1961). She was also a popular nightclub performer and gave her last stage performance

Marlene Dietrich was a star of both German and American films.

in 1974. After a period of retirement from the screen, she appeared in the film *Just a Gigolo* (1978). The documentary film *Marlene*, a review of her life and career, which included a voice-over interview of the star by Maximilian Schell, was released in 1986. Her autobiography, *Ich bin, Gott sei Dank, Berlinerin* ("I Am, Thank God, a Berliner"; Eng. trans. *Marlene*), was published in 1987. Eight years after her death, a collection of Dietrich's film costumes, recordings, written documents, photographs, and other personal items was put on permanent display in the Berlin Film Museum (2000).

Dietrich's persona was carefully crafted, and her films (with few exceptions) were skillfully executed. Although her vocal range was not great, her memorable renditions of songs such as *Falling in Love Again*, *Lili Marleen*, *La Vie en rose*, and *Give Me the Man* made them classics of an era. Her many affairs with both men and women were open secrets, but rather than destroying her career they seemed to enhance it. Her adoption of trousers and other mannish clothes made her a trendsetter and helped launch an American fashion style that persisted into the 21st century. In the words of the critic Kenneth Tynan: "She has sex, but no particular gender. She has the bearing of a man; the characters she plays love power and wear trousers. Her masculinity appeals to women and her sexuality to men." But her personal magnetism went far beyond her masterful androgynous image and her glamour; another of her admirers, the writer Ernest Hemingway, said, "If she had nothing more than her voice, she could break your heart with it."

SIMONE WEIL

(b. Feb. 3, 1909, Paris, France—d. Aug. 24, 1943, Ashford, Kent, Eng.)

The posthumously published works of Simone Weil, a French mystic, social philosopher, and activist in the French Resistance during World War II, had particular influence on French and English social thought.

Intellectually precocious, Weil also expressed social awareness at an early age. At five she refused sugar because the French soldiers at the front during World War I had none, and at six she was quoting the French dramatic poet Jean Racine (1639–99). In addition to studies in philosophy, classical philology, and science, Weil continued to embark on new learning projects as the need arose. She taught philosophy in several girls' schools from 1931 to 1938 and often became embroiled in conflicts with school boards as a result of her social activism, which entailed picketing, refusing to eat more than those on relief, and writing for leftist journals.

To learn the psychological effects of heavy industrial labor, she took a job in 1934–35 in an auto factory, where she observed the spiritually deadening effect of machines on her fellow workers. In 1936, she joined an Anarchist unit near Zaragoza, Spain, training for action in the Spanish Civil War, but after an accident in which she was badly scalded by boiling oil, she went to Portugal to recuperate. Soon thereafter, Weil had the first of several mystical experiences, and she subsequently came to view her social concerns as "ersatz Divinity." After the German occupation of Paris during World War II, Weil moved to the south of France, where she worked as a farm servant. She escaped with her parents to the United States in 1942 but then went to London to work with the French Resistance. To identify herself with her French compatriots under German occupation, Weil refused to eat more than the official ration in occupied France. Malnutrition and overwork led to a physical collapse, and during her hospitalization she was found to have tuberculosis. She died after a few months spent in a sanatorium.

Weil's writings, which were collected and published after her death, fill about 20 volumes. Her most important works are *La Pesanteur et la grâce* (1947; *Gravity and Grace*), a collection of religious essays and aphorisms; *L'Enracinement* (1949; *The Need for Roots*), an essay upon the obligations of the individual and the state; *Attente de Dieu* (1950; *Waiting for God*), a spiritual autobiography; *Oppression et Liberté* (1955; *Oppression and Liberty*), a collection of political and philosophical essays on war, factory work, language, and other topics; and three volumes of *Cahiers* (1951–56; *Notebooks*). Though born of Jewish parents, Weil eventually adopted a mystical theology that came very close to Roman Catholicism. A moral idealist committed to a vision of social justice, Weil in her writings explored her own religious life while also analyzing the individual's relation with the state and God, the spiritual shortcomings of modern industrial society, and the horrors of totalitarianism.

KATHERINE DUNHAM

(b. June 22, 1909, Glen Ellyn, Ill., U.S.—d. May 21, 2006, New York, N.Y.)

The American dancer, choreographer, and anthropologist Katherine Dunham was noted for her innovative interpretations of ritual and ethnic dances.

Dunham early became interested in dance. While a student at the University of Chicago, she formed a dance group that performed in concert at the Chicago World's Fair in 1934 and with the Chicago Civic Opera company in 1935–36. On graduating with a bachelor's degree in anthropology she undertook field studies in the Caribbean and in Brazil. By the time she received an MA from the University of Chicago, she had acquired a vast knowledge of the dances and rituals of the Black peoples of tropical America. (She later took a PhD in anthropology.) In 1938, she joined the Federal Theater Project in Chicago and composed a ballet, *L'Ag'Ya*, based on Caribbean dance. Two years later, she formed an all-Black company, which began touring extensively by 1943. *Tropics* (choreographed 1937) and *Le Jazz Hot* (1938) were among the earliest of many works that were based on her research.

Dunham was both a popular entertainer and a serious artist intent on tracing the roots of Black culture. Many of her students, trained in her studios in Chicago and New York City, became prominent in the field of modern dance. She choreographed for Broadway stage productions and opera—including *Aida* (1963) for the New York Metropolitan Opera. She also choreographed and starred in dance sequences in such films as *Carnival of Rhythm* (1942), *Stormy Weather* (1943), and *Casbah* (1947). In addition, Dunham conducted special projects for African American high school students in Chicago; was artistic and technical director (1966–67) to the president of Senegal; and served as artist-in-residence, and later professor, at Southern Illinois University, Edwardsville, and director of Southern Illinois's Performing Arts Training Center and Dynamic Museum in East Saint Louis, Illinois. Dunham was active in human rights causes, and in 1992 she staged a 47-day hunger strike to highlight the plight of Haitian refugees.

Dunham's writings, sometimes published under the pseudonym Kaye Dunn, include *Katherine Dunham's Journey to Accompong* (1946), an account of her anthropological studies in Jamaica; *A Touch of Innocence* (1959), an autobiography; *Island Possessed* (1969); and several articles for popular and scholarly journals. The recipient of numerous awards, Dunham received a Kennedy Center Honor in 1983 and the National Medal of Arts in 1989.

DOROTHY CROWFOOT HODGKIN

(b. May 12, 1910, Cairo, Egypt—d. July 29, 1994, Shipston-on-Stour, Warwickshire, Eng.)

The English chemist Dorothy Crowfoot Hodgkin determined the structure of penicillin and vitamin B_{12}, and her discoveries brought her the 1964 Nobel Prize for Chemistry.

Born Dorothy Mary Crowfoot, Hodgkin was the eldest of four sisters whose parents, John and Molly Crowfoot, worked in North Africa and the Middle East in colonial administration and later as archaeologists. Sent to England for their education, the girls spent much of their childhood apart from their parents. But it was their mother who especially encouraged Dorothy to pursue the passionate interest in crystals that she first displayed at age 10. Educated at a coeducational, state-funded secondary school in the small town of Beccles, Suffolk, Hodgkin fought to be allowed to study science along with the boys. She succeeded and was accepted in 1928 to read for a degree in chemistry at Somerville College, University of Oxford. As an undergraduate, she was one of the first to study the structure of an organic compound using X-ray crystallography.

Hodgkin moved to the University of Cambridge in 1932 to carry out doctoral research with British physicist John Desmond Bernal, who was to be a lifelong influence. In his laboratory, she extended work that he had begun on biological molecules, including sterols (the subject of her thesis), and helped him to make the first X-ray diffraction studies of pepsin, a crystalline protein. She was also highly receptive to his strongly pro-Soviet views and belief in the social function of science. Offered a temporary research fellowship at Somerville, one of Oxford's few colleges for women, she returned there in 1934 and remained until her retirement in 1977. (In the late 1940s the future prime minister Margaret Thatcher was one of her students.) Hodgkin established an X-ray laboratory in a corner of the Oxford University Museum of Natural History (better known for its dinosaur skeletons and mineral collections) and almost immediately began work taking X-ray photographs of insulin.

In 1937, she married the left-wing historian Thomas Hodgkin, who was then teaching adult-education classes in mining and industrial communities in the north of England. As his health was too poor for active military service, he continued this work throughout World War II, returning on weekends to Oxford where his wife remained working on penicillin. They had three children, born in 1938, 1941, and 1946. Thomas Hodgkin subsequently spent extended periods of time in West Africa, where he was an enthusiastic supporter and chronicler of the emerging postcolonial states. Following an infection after the birth of her first child, Dorothy Hodgkin developed chronic rheumatoid arthritis at age 28. This left her hands swollen and distorted, yet she continued to carry out the delicate manipulations necessary to mount and photograph the tiny crystals, smaller than a grain of salt, that she used in her studies.

Scientific Achievements

Hodgkin's insulin research was put to one side in 1939 when Australian pathologist Howard Florey and his colleagues at Oxford succeeded in isolating penicillin and asked her to solve its structure. By 1945, she had succeeded, describing the arrangement of its atoms in three dimensions. Penicillin was at that time the largest molecule to have succumbed to X-ray methods; moreover, the technique had resolved a dispute between eminent organic chemists about its structure. Hodgkin's work on penicillin was recognized by her election to the Royal Society, Britain's premier scientific academy, in 1947, only two years after a woman had been elected for the first time.

In the mid-1950s, Hodgkin discovered the structure of vitamin B_{12}; notably, she made extensive use of computers to carry out the complex computations involved. Her achievements led to her election in 1960 as the first Wolfson Research Professor of the Royal Society, a post she held while remaining in Oxford. Nominated more than once for the Nobel Prize, she won in 1964 for her work on penicillin and vitamin B_{12}. The following year, she was made a member of the Order of Merit, which is Britain's highest honor for achievement in science, the arts, and public life.

Hodgkin never gave up on discovering the structure of insulin, a large, complex protein molecule that could not be understood until both the techniques of X-ray diffraction and high-speed computing were sufficiently advanced. Eventually her patience was rewarded: working with an international team of young researchers, she discovered its structure in 1969, 34 years after she had taken her first X-ray photograph of an insulin crystal.

SOCIAL ACTIVISM

Hodgkin devoted much of the latter part of her life to the cause of scientists in developing countries, especially China and India, and to improved East-West relations and disarmament. From 1975 to 1988, she was president of the Pugwash Conferences on Science and World Affairs, an organization that brings together scientists from around the world to discuss peaceful progress toward international security and development. She also accepted the post of chancellor of the University of Bristol (1970–88), an honorary position in which she nevertheless fought vigorously for improved education funding at a time of government cutbacks. Only the steadily increasing pain and infirmity from her arthritis eventually forced her to curtail her public activities.

Hodgkin's soft-spoken, gentle, and modest demeanor hid a steely determination to achieve her ends, whatever obstacles might stand in her way. She inspired devotion in her students and colleagues, even the most junior of whom knew her simply as Dorothy. Her structural studies of biologically important molecules set standards for a field that was very much in development during her working life, and she made fundamental contributions to our understanding of how these molecules carry out their tasks in living systems.

MOTHER TERESA

(baptized Aug. 27, 1910, Skopje, Macedonia, Ottoman Empire [now in Republic of Macedonia]—d. Sept. 5, 1997, Calcutta [Kolkata], India; canonized Sept. 4, 2016)

Mother Teresa of Calcutta was the founder of the Order of the Missionaries of Charity, a Roman Catholic congregation of women dedicated to the poor, and particularly to the destitute of India. She was the recipient of numerous honors, including the 1979 Nobel Prize for Peace.

Mother Teresa was born Agnes Gonxha Bojaxhiu, the daughter of an ethnic Albanian grocer. In 1928, she went to Ireland to join the Sisters of Loretto at the Institute of the Blessed Virgin Mary and sailed only six weeks later to India as a teacher. She taught for 17 years at the order's school in Calcutta (Kolkata).

In 1946, Sister Teresa experienced her "call within a call," which she considered divine inspiration to devote herself to caring for the sick and poor. She then moved into the slums she had observed while teaching. Municipal authorities, upon her petition, gave her a pilgrim hostel, near the sacred temple of Kali, where she founded her order in 1948. Sympathetic companions soon flocked to her aid. Dispensaries and outdoor schools were organized. Mother Teresa adopted Indian citizenship, and her Indian nuns all donned the sari as their habit. In 1950, her order received canonical sanction from Pope Pius XII, and in 1965 it became a pontifical congregation (subject only to the pope). In 1952, she established Nirmal Hriday ("Place for the Pure of Heart"), a hospice where the terminally ill could die with dignity. Her order also opened numerous centers serving the blind, the aged, and the disabled. Under Mother Teresa's guidance, the Missionaries of Charity built a leper colony, called Shanti Nagar ("Town of Peace"), near Asansol, India.

In 1963, the Indian government awarded Mother Teresa the title Padmashri ("Lord of the Lotus") for her services to the people of India. In 1964, on his trip to India, Pope Paul VI gave her his ceremonial limousine, which she immediately raffled to help finance her leper colony. In 1968, she was summoned to Rome to found a home there, staffed primarily with Indian nuns. In recognition of her apostolate, she was honored on January 6, 1971, by Pope Paul, who awarded her the first Pope John XXIII Peace Prize. In 1979, she received the Nobel Peace Prize for her humanitarian work.

In her later years Mother Teresa spoke out against divorce, contraception, and abortion. She also suffered ill health and had a heart attack in 1989. In 1990, she resigned as head of the order but was returned to office by a near unanimous vote—the lone dissenting voice was her own. A worsening heart condition forced her retirement, and the order chose the Indian-born Sister Nirmala as her

Mother Teresa was canonized and named a saint by the Roman Catholic church in 2016, 19 years after her death.

successor in 1997. At the time of Mother Teresa's death, her order included hundreds of centers in more than 90 countries with some 4,000 nuns and hundreds of thousands of lay workers. Within two years of Mother Teresa's death, the process to declare her a saint was begun, and Pope John Paul II issued a special dispensation to expedite the process of canonization. She was beatified on October 19, 2003, reaching the ranks of the blessed in what was then the shortest time in the history of the church. She was canonized by Pope Francis I on September 4, 2016.

Although Mother Teresa displayed cheerfulness and a deep commitment to God in her daily work, her letters (which were collected and published in 2007) indicate that she did not feel God's presence in her soul during the last 50 years of her life. The letters reveal the suffering she endured and her feeling that Jesus had abandoned her at the start of her mission. Continuing to experience a spiritual darkness, she came to believe that she was sharing in Christ's Passion, particularly the moment in which Christ asks, "My God, my God, why have you forsaken me?" Despite this hardship, Mother Teresa integrated the feeling of absence into her daily religious life and remained committed to her faith and her work for Christ.

Glossary

anodyne: Something that soothes or comforts.

bourgeoisie: The middle class of society.

destitute: Suffering from extreme poverty.

disconsolate: Very sad.

fascism: A political system headed by a dictator in which opposition is not permitted.

femme fatale: A seductive, mysterious, and sometimes dangerous woman.

haute couture: The houses or designers that create fashion trends.

jettison: To discard.

kibbutz: A communal farm or settlement in Israel.

paean: A song of joy, praise, or triumph.

posthumously: Occurring after the death of a person.

sanatorium: An establishment that provides medical care and various treatments for the improvement of health.

suffrage: The right to vote.

tedious: Boring.

For More Information

BOOKS
Bried, Erin. *Noisemakers: 25 Women Who Raised Their Voices and Changed the World.* New York, NY: Alfred A. Knopf, 2020.

Cooper, Ilene. *Eleanor Roosevelt, Fighter for Justice: Her Impact on the Civil Rights Movement, the White House, and the World.* New York, NY: Abrams Books for Young Readers, 2019.

Fleming, Candace. *Amelia Lost: The Life and Disappearance of Amelia Earhart.* New York, NY: Yearling, 2019.

Murray, Laura K. *Mother Teresa.* Mankato, MN: Creative Education and Creative Paperbacks, 2019.

WEBSITES
Coco Chanel: Modernism
www.artsandculture.google.com/story/rQWBy_v7yDpuIg
The Metropolitan Museum of Art presents an overview of Chanel's fashion innovations and their influence with images of her designs.

Katherine Dunham: A Life in Dance
www.loc.gov/item/ihas.200152685/
This page from the Library of Congress discusses Dunham's life and contains videos of her Haitian dance demonstrations.

The Kennedy Center
www.kennedy-center.org/education/resources-for-educators/classroom-resources/media-and-interactives/media/dance/martha-graham--appalachian-spring/
You can read a brief biography of Martha Graham and watch footage of her choreography for Appalachian Spring on this website.

The Nobel Prize
www.nobelprize.org
Learn about the prestigious awards presented for world-changing accomplishments and find short biographies of the people—such as Irène Joliot-Curie, Dorothy Crowfoot Hodgkin, and Mother Teresa—who won them.

INDEX

African Americans, 29, 53–54
anthropology, 53
Arab-Israeli wars, 47

ballet, 33, 35–37, 54
birth control, 6–7, 59

chemistry, 42–45, 55–58
China, 37–40, 57

dancers, 32–37, 53–54
depression, 9, 11, 21

England, 6–7, 7–23, 55–58

fascism, 19–21, 44, 49
fashion, 23–24, 51
first lady, 25–30
France, 23–24, 42–45, 52–53
French Resistance, 52

Germany, 30–31, 44, 47, 48–51

Hitler, Adolf, 21, 49
human rights, 29, 54

India, 18, 57, 58–61
Israel, 45–48

Medal of Freedom, 37
modern dance, 32–37, 54
Modernism, 18, 22–23
mysticism, 33, 52–53

Nazis, 44, 49
Nobel Prize, 42–43, 55, 57–58

novels, 7, 10, 12–23

penicillin, 55–57
perfume, 24
plays, 19–21
Post-Impressionism, 10, 15
presidents (U.S.), 25, 27, 29
psychoanalysis, 30–32

radioactivity, 42–43

saint, 58–61
same-sex relationships, 15, 51
Spanish Civil War, 20, 44, 52
suicide, 11, 16, 21

Taiwan, 39–40
tuberculosis, 30, 53

United Nations, 25, 29
United States, 25–30, 31–32, 32–37, 39, 40–42, 49, 52, 53–54
Universal Declaration of Human Rights, 29

World War I, 26, 40, 52
World War II, 7, 21, 24, 39, 45, 52, 56

X-rays, 55–57